The name Star Bright Books and the Star Bright Books logo are registered
trademarks of Star Bright Books, Inc. Please visit: www.starbrightbooks.com.
For bulk orders, please email: orders@starbrightbooks.com, or
call customer service at: (617) 354-1300.

Animal Facts by India Futterman

Printed on paper from sustainable forests

Hardcover ISBN-13: 978-1-59572-710-7
Paperback ISBN-13: 978-1-59572-711-4
Star Bright Books / MA / 00109150
Printed in China / WKT / 0 9 8 7 6 5 4 3 2 1

Library of Congress Cataloging-in-Publication Data is available

*"With lots of love to my grandchildren,
who inspired this book through our many
walks enjoying nature together."* —J.H.

*"My Mum Peggy, and Elise and Mya
my Granddaughters"* — M.C.

# GRANDMA
## *is a* SLOWPOKE

BY
**JANET HALFMANN**

ILLUSTRATED BY
**MICHELE COXON**

**STAR BRIGHT BOOKS**
Cambridge, Massachusetts

I like going for a walk with my grandma.
But she is a slowpoke.

We hear a bird singing.

We stop and look.
"Those are cardinals," says Grandma.

"Listen, it says,
*Wheet, wheet, wheet.*"
We whistle back,
"*Wheet, wheet, wheet.*"

We walk a few more steps.
Grandma stops.
She is a slowpoke.

Grandma kneels on the ground.
"Look at the big seed that ant is carrying," she says.
I bend down to take a closer look. That ant is strong!

We walk some more.
Grandma stops.
She is a slowpoke.
"Shhhhhhhh," she whispers.
Grandma points to rabbits in the grass.

We stay as still as the rabbits for a long time.

We walk again. Grandma stops.
She is a slow poke.
"Look," Grandma says, pointing.
"There is a squirrel's nest way up high."

I look up.
What a fun place to live!
Two squirrels run down the tree.

Grandma stops on a bridge.
She is a slowpoke.

"Look at that duck splashing,"
says Grandma.
"He is taking a bath."
I laugh. I didn't know ducks
take baths.

We walk along the stream.
Grandma stops again.
She is a slowpoke.

"Look how the baby geese swim between their mom and dad," she says. We count the babies.

We walk some more.

Then I spot something that Grandma doesn't notice.

I point to a furry animal swimming in the water.

Grandma stops and looks.
"It's a muskrat," she says.
"They live along the riverbank."

We watch the muskrats until they disappear.
Then Grandma says, "It's time to start for
home. Soon it will be getting dark."
But I am not ready to go.
I want to see the muskrats again.

"Okay, we can stay," says Grandma.
"But only until the fireflies come out."

We watch and wait for the muskrats
but they never come back.

The fireflies begin to glow.
They shine here and there,
then everywhere.

"Time to go, slowpoke," says Grandma.
We start for home.

"What took so long?" asks Mom.
"We saw so-o-o-o-o much!" I say.

"It was fun being slowpokes together."

# Animal Facts

### Cardinals

You probably know cardinals by their bright red color, but did you know that only male cardinals are red? Females are light brown with a reddish tinge on the wings, tail, and crest and a red beak. While cardinals tend to hide their nests in trees and shrubs, they'll likely visit your own backyard–especially if you provide them with sunflower seeds in a bird feeder.

### Ants

Ants live and work in large groups, with different ants doing different jobs–workers, soldiers, and queens that lay eggs–to serve the community. An ant colony, also called a formicary, may exist in a network of underground tunnels, on pieces of decaying wood, or within an anthill. There are over 8,800 known ant species. Some ants can carry things up to 100 times their body weight!

### Rabbits

Maybe you've caught a glimpse of an eastern cottontail, the most common rabbit in North America. They can travel between 10 and 15 feet with each hop, or up to 18 miles per hour! Rabbits are herbivores which means they eat only plants. Cottontails are most active at night but you may see them in the evening and at dawn.

### Squirrels

Look up into a tree with a hole in its trunk and you might spot a family of squirrels has made its home there. Squirrels also construct nests of leaves on branches if they can't find a suitable hole in a tree trunk. Squirrels eat acorn seeds and other hard nuts that wear their teeth down, which is why their teeth never stop growing!

### Ducks and Geese

Ducks and geese are both part of the bird family. Most ducks and geese choose a partner before mating season and remain together for a long time. They always nest near the water, and their chicks are able to walk and swim within hours of hatching!

### Muskrats

Muskrats are mainly nocturnal–active at night–mammals that make their homes in ponds, rivers, lakes, and streams. They often build dens by digging tunnels on the banks of rivers and streams, and they live in the burrows that they've created. Muskrats also build lodges in the water using sticks and stems, much like beavers do.

### Fireflies

How do fireflies light up? This kind of light is called bioluminescence. Fireflies are not the only creatures that have the ability to produce light–certain fish and worms do the same! Some types of firefly have their own unique pattern of light flashes, allowing them to identify others of their species.